The Pinkish, Purplish, Bluish Egg

written and illustrated by BILL PEET

HOUGHTON MIFFLIN COMPANY BOSTON

Manufactured in China.

LIBRARY OF CONGRESS CATALOG CARD NUMBER: 63-7328

ISBN 0-395-18472-X
ISBN 0-395-36172-9 PAP

SCP 30

Myrtle was sad and completely depressed
As she sat staring down at her empty dove nest;
Her children had flown off and left her that day.
It was hard on a mother to send them away,
But her instincts had told her that they were full-grown
And ready to start on a life of their own.
She held back her tears for as long as she could
Till they'd flown out of sight on their way through the wood.

Then she fluttered far back in a dark cave to brood
And try to get over her miserable mood.
As she swooped through the gloom with a woebegone sigh,
An odd-colored oval-shaped rock caught her eye.
But Myrtle, on closer inspection, could tell
That the rock was an egg, for it had an eggshell.
"I must hatch it!" she cried, "or at least try my best—
If there's some way to get it back up to my nest."

This problem of Myrtle's was solved right away
By some frisky young squirrels who'd come there to play.
They took off with the egg in a wild free-for-all,
Sent it bouncing along like a big bowling ball.
Out of the cave door, across the rough ground,
And straight for the tree it went whirling around,
And to Myrtle's surprise, in less than a minute
They were up to her nest, and plunked the egg in it.

Soon all sorts of birds began flocking around
To see the big egg that Myrtle had found—
Blue jays and redbirds and noisy magpies
And a big stuffy owl who was worldly and wise.
"It won't hatch," said the owl. "That egg is stone-cold.
Why, for all that we know it's a thousand years old."
"If it does hatch," a jay said, "I'll bet it's a turtle,
For, after all, you are a turtledove, Myrtle."
But the dove didn't listen to what the birds said;
She was bound and determined to go right ahead.

Early one day when no birds were around,
Myrtle awoke to a faint scratching sound.
It came from inside of the egg; she could tell
Something was trying to break through the shell.
"I knew it! I knew it!" she gleefully cried.
"The egg's going to hatch! There is someone inside!"

And once more the birds crowded Myrtle's treetop
To watch as the egg cracked apart with a pop.
Then a feathery thing poked his little head out.
Bewildered and frightened, he looked all about.
"Happy birthday!" the dove whispered softly to him
And he felt more at home and hopped out on the limb.

At first all the birds were just too stunned to speak.
But finally a jay blurted out, "It's a freak!
Just look! The thing is half lion, half eagle.
I'm sure that it must be unsafe or illegal."

"No, no," said the owl, with a long, thoughtful look.
"It's a creature straight out of a fairy-tale book.
The thing's called a griffin. It doesn't exist,
But as a precaution I firmly insist
That we ought to get rid of the brute right away
Or it might grow up and cause trouble someday."

This was too much for Myrtle; fire flashed in her eyes
And she ruffled her feathers to look twice her size.
"You old coot!" she exploded. "You mixed-up old bird!
That's the silliest thing anyone's ever heard.
If a griffin's not real, then how under the sun
Can a nothing-at-all ever harm anyone?"
With a furious charge like a mad bumblebee
She chased the owl back to his old hollow tree.

The commotion and noise made him so terrified
That the griffin crawled back in his eggshell to hide.
Myrtle called softly, "Come out, it's all clear,
The birds have all gone, I'm the only one here."

So the griffin crept out on the tree limb once more
With slightly more courage than he'd had before.
"That's better," said Myrtle. "Now the first thing we'll do
Is pick out a name that sounds just right for you.
There's an old Bible name that I think rhymes with meek.
I know! It's Ezekiel. For short that is Zeke.

“And now Zeke if you’d like I will teach you to fly
You’ve a fine pair of wings, let’s give it a try.
But first,” she continued, “you’d better watch me.”
And she sailed a short distance away from the tree.
It seemed very simple and easy to him
So Zeke spread his wings and sailed straight off the limb.
For a minute it looked like a pretty good start
Until, all of a sudden, down went his hind part.

He fought his way frantically back through the air
And just reached the limb, but with not much to spare.
"Your last half," sighed Myrtle, "doesn't seem to be trying.
It has no natural instincts, no interest in flying.
But don't worry, Zeke, leave that end up to me.
I have an idea that will work, wait and see."

Then by holding his long lion tail in her beak,
Myrtle supported the last half of Zeke
And the griffin went gliding along on the breeze
While the dove gently steered him around through the trees.
As they went sailing past, the owl hooted and sneered
While the mockingbirds mocked and the blue jays all jeered.
But the dove didn't care, she expected them to;
That's always the way when you try something new.

This first flight of Zeke's was a very short hop;
Before long they made a refueling stop.
Then Myrtle went bustling around on the ground
To show him just where the best bird food was found.

In crumbling old stumps they found grubworms and slugs
And under flat rocks they found swarms of fat bugs.
"Sowbugs," said Myrtle, "have vitamin A
And so you should eat quite a few every day.
But don't overeat, that's a wise old bird rule;
A flyer who gains too much weight is a fool."
So while Myrtle was teaching her Zeke how to fly,
She gave him a set of good rules to live by.

At the end of each day Zeke would stretch out to rest
High on the tree limb beside Myrtle's nest.
And softly she'd coo an old dove lullaby
While he dreamily stared at the moon drifting by,
For Myrtle had said, "If you look for a while
You can see the moon's face with its bright happy smile."
And in this way he fell off to sleep very soon,
Trying to make out the face on the moon.

When spring came again Zeke had reached his full size;
He turned out to be huge which was no big surprise.
What amazed everyone was his skill as a flyer,
For that is the thing all the birds most admire.
"He's a marvel," said Myrtle with a satisfied smile,
"And he flies as you see in the classic dove style."
"He flies too well," the owl said, "to suit me,"
As he quivered and quaked in his old hollow tree.
"And if we're ever attacked by that powerful brute
Our chance of escape wouldn't be worth a hoot."

Myrtle tried to ignore what the old owl had said
But she couldn't quite put it all out of her head.
So wherever Zeke went, the dove followed along
Just to make sure that he did nothing wrong.

Late one afternoon as they wandered around
They passed by the cave where the egg had been found.
"Now that's strange," said Zeke as he peeked in the door,
"I have a feeling I've been here before.
It's just the right place for a big brute like me.
Besides I'm too big now to sleep in a tree."
"If you sleep here," said Myrtle with a shiver of fright,
"Foxes and wolves might surprise you some night.
They're bloodthirsty creatures," the dove pointed out,
"And there's no telling when they'll come prowling about."

One night as the griffin stretched out on the limb
Zeke felt as if someone were staring at him,
And there, sure enough, down below on the ground,
The foxes and wolves had come prowling around.
Somehow they'd heard of the fabulous beast
So they were all set for a fabulous feast.
And Zeke was so worried for fear he might fall,
For the rest of that night he slept hardly at all.

He awoke the next day with a fierce eagle scowl
And from deep in his throat came a low lion growl.
"I could tear all those scoundrels to ribbons," snarled Zeke,
"With these great eagle claws and this powerful beak."
This came as a shock to the delicate dove,
The symbol of peace and of motherly love,
And she tearfully pleaded with Zeke not to do it.
"I'd die," Myrtle moaned, "I couldn't live through it.
Violence is wrong and it's sinful I say.
If you'll only be patient they might go away."

But they weren't going to leave for all Zeke could see
And he just couldn't stand one more night in the tree.
So Zeke left the woods and sailed off through the sky
While Myrtle was chasing a big dragonfly.

When he finally decided he'd gone far enough
He went gliding down to roost on a bluff
Overlooking a region so bleak and so bare
That only the vultures could stand living there.

“This place,” said Zeke, “is as strange as can be
So maybe it’s meant for a creature like me.
But I couldn’t stand living out here in these rocks;
It’s a much better place for a wolf or a fox.”
Then all of a sudden he sat up with a jerk.
“Why, there’s an idea,” he said, “that might work!”
And he hurried along toward the woods at top speed,
Anxious to see if his plan might succeed.

When he came to the forest Zeke dropped from the sky
With a loud lion roar that was part eagle cry.
All the birds were astounded and so terrified
That they went streaking off in the bushes to hide.

But the foxes and wolves all came running out
To see what the unearthly noise was about
And were swept off their feet, jerked up by the tail,
Then over the treetops the scoundrels set sail,
Helplessly howling and wailing with fright,
For this, you see, was their very first flight.

Zeke made the long trip without dropping one fox
And set them down gently on one of the rocks.
Then as he departed the griffin called out,
"That'll teach you scoundrels to go prowling about.
If you ever come back to the woods, don't forget
I'll take all of you on a much longer trip yet."

When Zeke told the dove about what he had done
She was so very proud of her gigantic son
That she scurried about as fast as she could
To tell every bird in that part of the wood.
And now at last there wasn't one doubt
But what the fierce griffin they'd worried about
Was a peace-loving creature and tame as could be.
Why, even the owl finally had to agree.

"But I'm right," the owl said, "on one thing at least;
He doesn't exist, he's a mythical beast."
"Does he mean," worried Zeke, "that I'm not really here?
That most any minute I might disappear?"
"It's nonsense," scoffed Myrtle, "he's a silly old bird.
But if it makes him feel better, let him have the last word."